THIS IGLOO BOOK BELONGS TO:

igloobooks

Published in 2022
First published in the UK by Igloo Books Ltd
An imprint of Igloo Books Ltd
Cottage Farm, NN6 0BJ, UK
Owned by Bonnier Books
Sveavägen 56, Stockholm, Sweden
www.igloobooks.com

0522 001
2 4 6 8 10 9 7 5 3 1
ISBN 978-1-80022-572-5

Written by Stephanie Moss
Illustrated by Hannah McCaffery

Designed by Jason Shortland
Edited by Claire Mowat

Printed and manufactured in China

BABY SHARK
SUPERHERO

igloobooks

Beneath the waves, under the sea,
Baby Shark plays happily.

But then, what's that?

A glint,

a gleam.

He can't **believe** what he has seen!

His **super-strength** grows from within...

... and he gets **super-speedy** fins.

He says,
"I don't know what to do.

I need a superhero crew!"

He races faster than the tide
and asks Crab,

"Please, fight by my side?"

A duo? **No!**
They need one more.

KER-SPLASH!

They dash up to the shore.

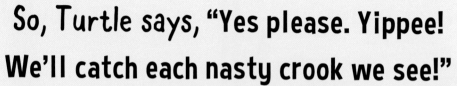

So, Turtle says, "Yes please. Yippee!
We'll catch each nasty crook we see!"

While seaweed sways...

... and bubbles pop...

KAZAP!

They put crime to a stop.

When darkness falls, their friends all sleep.
They capture bad guys of the deep.

"Three cheers for Baby Shark. Woo-hoo!"
They say, "We're all safe, thanks to you."

While Baby Shark
parades the town,
both Crab and Turtle
start to frown.

"That's it!" they say.
So, late that night,
they seek the oyster's
magic light.

With super-strength and sight and speed...

... they plan a super
bad-guy deed.

Baby Shark sees water whirling,
smashing homes, it keeps on swirling.

BLAM!

He works until he's won,
and then his powers
are all gone.

Confused and sad, our hero leaves,
then sees something he can't believe.

With tears of sadness, they admit,
they didn't like his fame one bit.

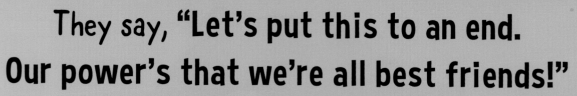

They say, "Let's put this to an end.
Our power's that we're all best friends!"